Sylvie Jones

Who's in the Tub?

Pictures by

Pascale Constantin

BLUE APPLE BOOKS

"Willy John Jones,
are you in the tub?

"Willy John Jones,
I'd rather not shout.

The sooner you're in,
the sooner you're out."

"MOM,
I HEAR YOU.

"Willy, I do not hear a single splash.
I don't believe that you're in that bath."

"Then finish up, Willy.

It's getting late.

I want you in bed
no later than eight."

"Aw, Mom, one more minute.

"Willy, did I hear you say WE?"